Penguin

SUNDIATA THE LION KING
AND OTHER
ROYAL TALES

LEVEL

RETOLD BY HELEN HOLWILL
ILLUSTRATED BY HANNAH TOLSON, LIDIA TOMASHEVSKAYA,
PHAM QUANG PHUC AND ALHETEIA STRAATHOF
SERIES EDITOR: SORREL PITTS

PENGUIN BOOKS

UK | USA | Canada | Ireland | Australia
India | New Zealand | South Africa

Penguin Books is part of the Penguin Random House group of companies
whose addresses can be found at global.penguinrandomhouse.com.

www.penguin.co.uk   www.puffin.co.uk   www.ladybird.co.uk

Ladybird Tales of Crowns and Thrones first published by Ladybird Books Ltd, 2020
This Penguin Readers edition published 2021
001

Copyright © Ladybird Books Ltd, 2020, 2021
Original stories retold by Yvonne Battle-Felton ("Sundiata the Lion King",
"Yennenga and the Mossi Kingdom")
and Chitra Soundar ("Rostam and Rakhsh", "Shakuntala")
Text for Penguin Readers edition adapted by Helen Holwill
"Sundiata the Lion King" illustrated by Hannah Tolson
"Yennenga and the Mossi Kingdom" illustrated by Lidia Tomashevskaya
"Rostam and his horse Rakhsh" illustrated by Pham Quang Phuc
"Shakuntala and the gold ring" illustrated by Alheteia Straathof

Text for Penguin Readers edition copyright © Penguin Books Ltd, 2021
Cover illustrations copyright © Penguin Books Ltd, 2020

Printed in China

The authorised representative in the EEA is Penguin Random House Ireland,
Morrison Chambers, 32 Nassau Street, Dublin D02 YH68.

A CIP catalogue record for this book is available from the British Library

ISBN: 978-0-241-49313-7

All correspondence to:
Penguin Books
Penguin Random House Children's
One Embassy Gardens, 8 Viaduct Gardens
London SW11 7BW

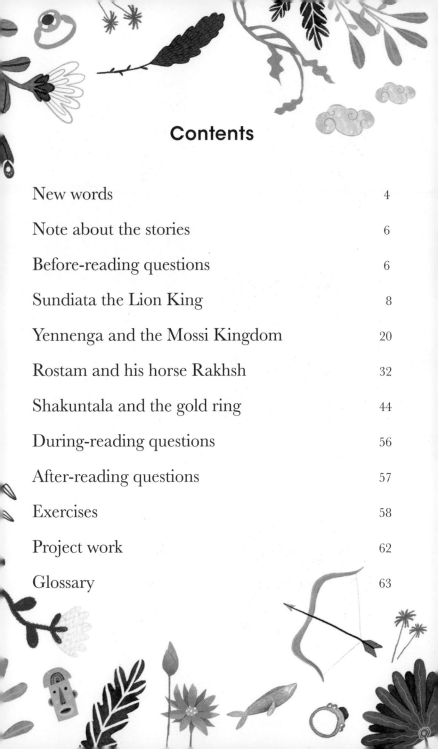

Contents

New words

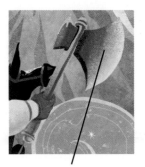

axe

bow and arrow

deer

elephant

forest

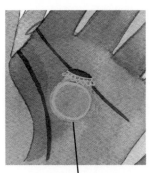

gold ring

king

lion

mountain

queen

sword

warrior

Note about the stories

Families everywhere in the world are different, and they all have their problems. The same is true for **royal families***, too.

The people in these four stories come from different places. They come from Mali, Ghana, Persia and India. But they have many of the same hopes and problems. Their **kingdoms** and their people are very important to them. They have to be **brave**, and they often have to fight for their family or kingdom.

Before-reading questions

1 Does your country have a royal family? What are their names? Do you like royal families?

2 Make two lists in your notebook with the words from the "New words" pages. You can call the lists "Words I know" and "Words I need to learn".

3 Look at the "Contents" page and the titles of the stories. What is going to happen in the four stories, do you think?

*Definitions of words in **bold** can be found in the glossary on pages 63–64.

SUNDIATA
THE
LION KING
AND OTHER
ROYAL TALES

Sundiata the Lion King

King Konaté and his wife, Queen Sassouma, lived in the **kingdom** of Manding, Africa. They had a beautiful **palace** and their young son, Dankaran, played happily there. But one day, a **fortune teller** came to see the king.

"A woman called Sogolon is going to have a son," said the man. "And this boy will be a wonderful king."

"What?" said the king. "But **Prince** Dankaran will be the next king!"

"Maybe he will be king one day," answered the fortune teller. "But Sogolon's son will be a stronger and more famous king. He will bring money to this kingdom and make it great."

The king loved his wife. But he did not want the next king to be another man's son. He thought for a long time. Then he asked Sogolon to come to the palace and marry him. He wanted her child to be his son.

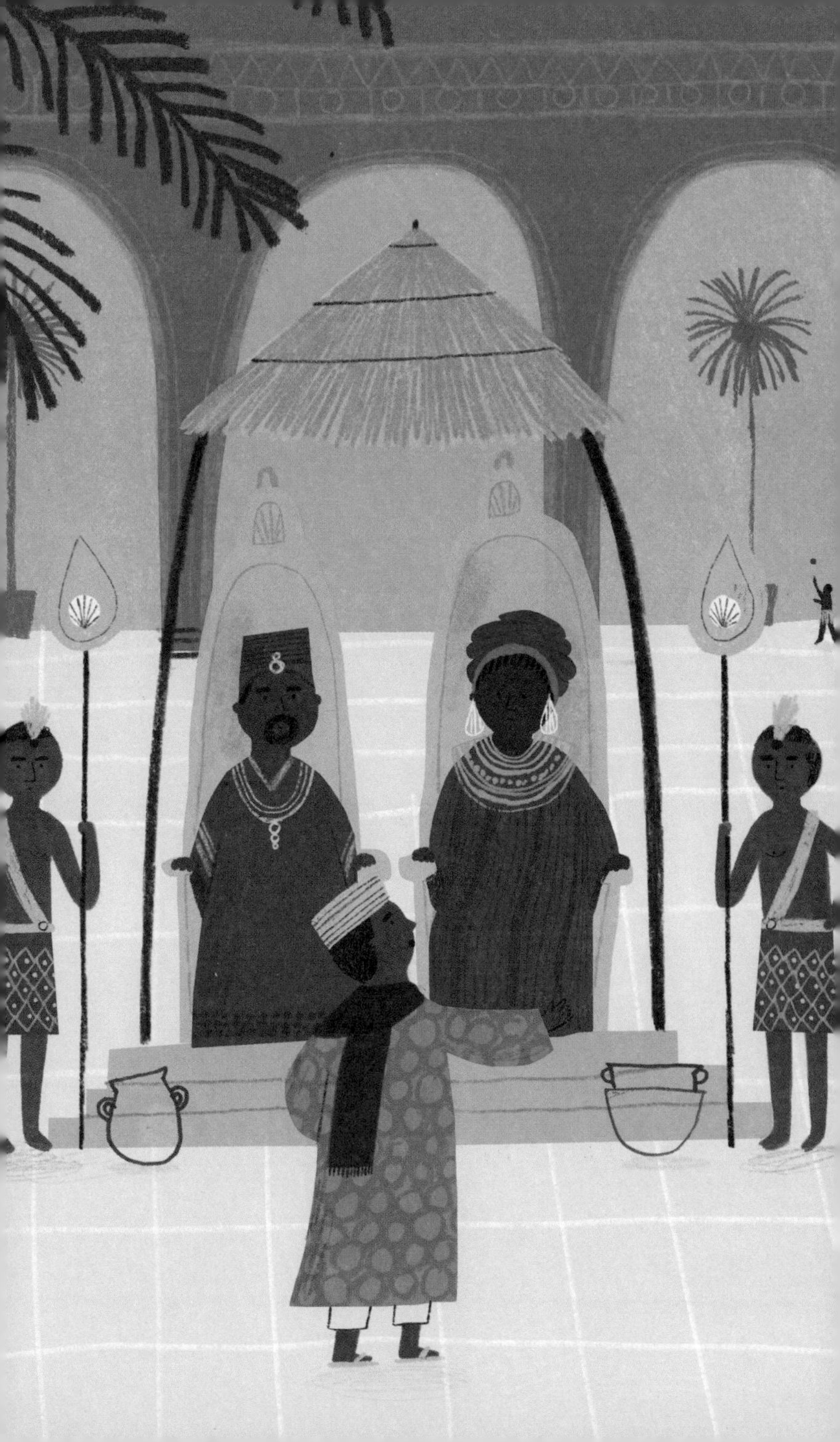

Months later, Sogolon had a baby, and they called him Sundiata. But the baby was very small and thin.

"This baby isn't strong! How will he be a great king?" said the king.

Sundiata was a small child, and he often was not well. Everyone laughed at him because he could not walk. Then an important day came. At seven years old, boys changed into men. On this day, Sundiata wanted to walk in front of the Manding people. His mother gave him two very strong walking sticks. Sundiata started to stand, but the sticks **broke**. People wanted to help him, but he said no. Then, for the first time, he stood and walked!

The Manding people were very happy.

"Sundiata can walk!" they said. "He is as strong as a lion!"

Sundiata grew very strong, and he learned to be a warrior.

"My son is strong, and he will be a great king!" said his father. Dankaran was very angry about this. "The first son is always king!" he thought.

Then King Konaté died, and Dankaran wanted to be king. He visited a **sorcerer**.

One evening, Sundiata saw the sorcerer.

"Hello!" Sundiata said. The man stopped but did not speak. "What do you want?" the boy asked. "Would you like my elephant?" But again the man said nothing.

"You want to kill me," Sundiata said, quietly. "Am I right? Do it now, and do it quickly."

"This boy is so kind and friendly," thought the sorcerer. "I cannot kill him."

"Run," he told Sundiata. "Leave Manding. Dankaran wants to kill you, and he will look for you."

Sundiata talked to his mother and his sister, Nyakhaleng. "We must leave Manding now!" he said. That day they left their home.

Sundiata, Sogolon and Nyakhaleng travelled for seven long years. They visited many villages, but no one wanted them to stay. "Dankaran is very angry with Sundiata," the villagers said. "We must not make him angry with us, too!"

In the seventh year, Sundiata and his mother and sister stayed in a village called Djedeba. Then one day, the king there asked Sundiata to come to his palace.

"Let's play a game," said King Mansa to Sundiata. "But you must **win** the game. Or you will die."

Sundiata looked at the swords on the wall. "I want to win, and then you must give me that big long sword."

"Yes, I will give you the sword," said the king. "But it's a difficult game."

They started to play the game, and the king began to tell a story about a young warrior.

"I know the end of the story," said Sundiata. "The money came yesterday."

King Mansa stopped and looked at Sundiata. How did he know about the money?

"My father's first wife, Sassouma, gave you some money. And now you have to kill someone. Is that it?" Sundiata said.

Sundiata was right. The king planned to kill him.

The king stopped the game and said, "Leave

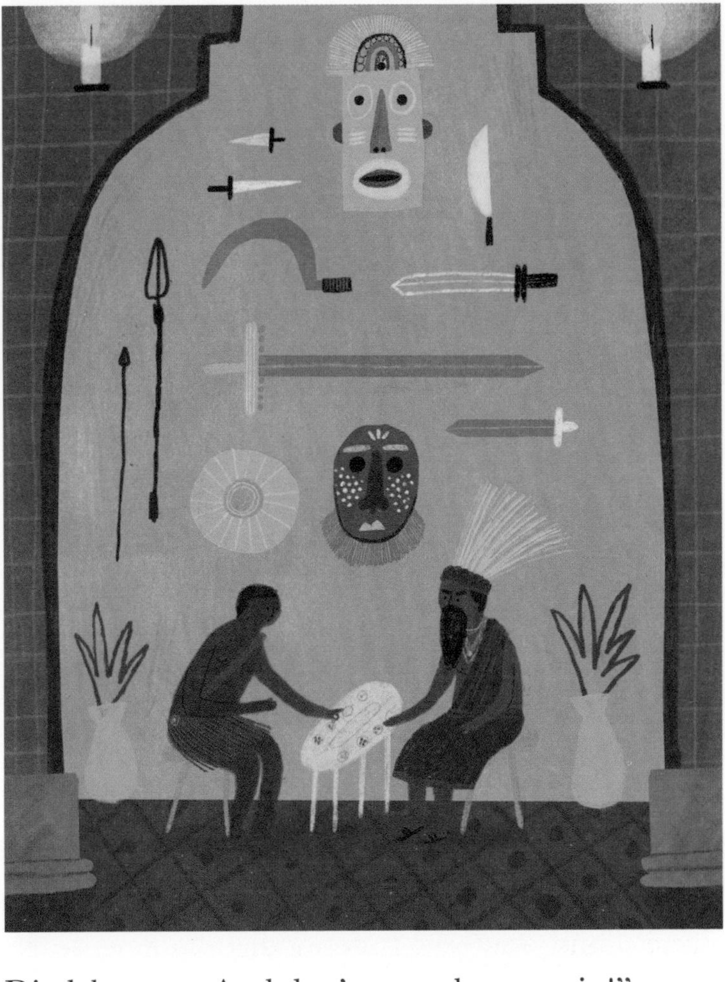

Djedeba now. And don't come here again!"

Sundiata and his family travelled again until they arrived in Mema. They stayed there for many years. But one day a man came to speak to Sundiata.

"I have bad news from Manding," said the man. "Your brother Dankaran was king, but the sorcerer Sumanguru killed him. Your other brother was then king, and he died, too. You are as strong and as **brave** as a lion. Please come home because the Manding people need you."

"No, my mother is not well. I cannot leave her," said Sundiata.

But his mother wanted him to go. "Leave me here," she said. "Your people are important. Go to them."

Sundiata was sad to leave his mother, but she was right. The next day, Sundiata and Nyakhaleng started to walk to Manding. After a long time, they arrived at Dakhajala. It was the city next to Manding.

"I am going to fight Sumanguru. Will you help me?" Sundiata asked the people of Dakhajala.

"Yes!" they answered. But the fight was very difficult because Sumanguru was a strong sorcerer. He fought with **magic**, not swords.

Nyakhaleng wanted to help her brother. She thought of a good plan. The next day, she quietly visited the sorcerer, Sumanguru.

"My brother doesn't want me," she told Sumanguru. "Can I stay with you?" Sumanguru liked Nyakhaleng, and he said yes.

"People call my brother the lion king," said Nyakhaleng, "but he's not strong. He only walked without walking sticks!"

Sumanguru laughed. "Sundiata can't kill me," he said. "And I have my father's magic, too. My father lives in a **cave** in the mountains. I cannot die until he dies!"

"Sumanguru is strong because of his father's magic!" thought Nyakhaleng. She went to her brother and told him this news. The next day, Sundiata went with his warriors to the mountains. They found the old sorcerer's cave and Sundiata killed him with his great sword.

The magic was gone and Sumanguru was not strong any more. He changed into a bird and flew up into the sky. No one saw him again. The people were very happy, and they smiled and shouted. Sundiata was now the first king of Mali.

The fortune teller was right. Sundiata was a strong, brave king and his people loved him.

Yennenga and the Mossi Kingdom

The people of Dagomba, in Africa, loved the young **Princess** Yennenga. Her father, King Nedega, was a good king. He taught Yennenga to be kind and to help the Dagomba people.

She often carried water, **looked after** younger children, or helped older people. She was also very good at working on farms. She loved to look after the **crops** and watch them grow.

Yennenga had a beautiful, strong horse, and she rode it every day. She was a wonderful rider, and she could go as fast as the wind. She rode and **trained** her horse a lot.

"Why do you train so hard?" her brothers asked. "You won't be able to be a warrior and fight because you are a girl. Father will always say no. You must stay here, at home."

Yennenga did not listen to her brothers. She rode faster and faster and trained hard every day.

Now Yennenga was the fastest rider in the Dagbon Kingdom.

Then she started to use a sword and a bow and arrow. A year later, Yennenga went to see her father.

"Father, the Malinke people are coming closer every day and we must fight them," she said. "I am your fastest rider and I am very brave. I can use a sword and a bow and arrow. My brothers are going to fight with you, and I want to go with them. Can I go?"

The king thought for a long time. His daughter trained hard, and she was stronger than her brothers. But she was also very kind and gave the most help to the Dagomba people.

"You cannot come because then there will be no one here," he said. "Who will look after our people?"

"We must all fight to win this **battle**," answered Yennenga. "We have to win. Or there will be no kingdom to look after."

From that day, Yennenga went to all the battles and her father was very happy with her.

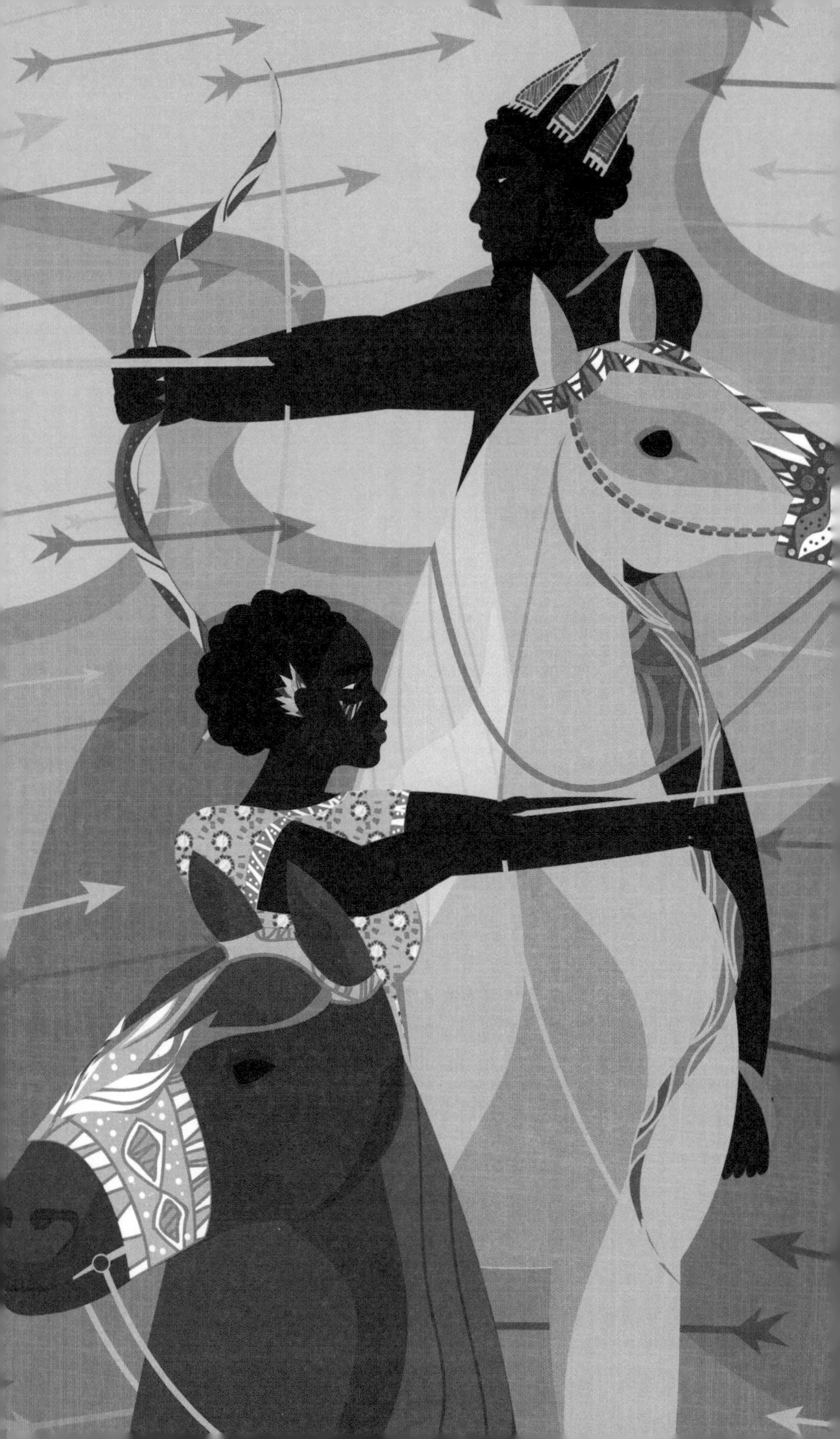

Yennenga was a brave warrior, and she won many battles. But she travelled a lot and was not often at home with her people. One day she went to talk to her father.

"Father, I am a good warrior, and I had to fight. But now the Malinke people are quiet, and they don't want to fight us. Can I go home now and look after my people?"

The king was angry. "You wanted to be a warrior, but now you want to stop! The Malinke people will see that, and they will fight us again."

"But my brothers are here, and they are good warriors. I want to go home and look after our people," said Yennenga. "They need me."

"No," answered the king. "I need you more than the people need you. Never talk about this again."

Years went by and Yennenga was very sad. Then one day, she started to grow crops outside her father's door.

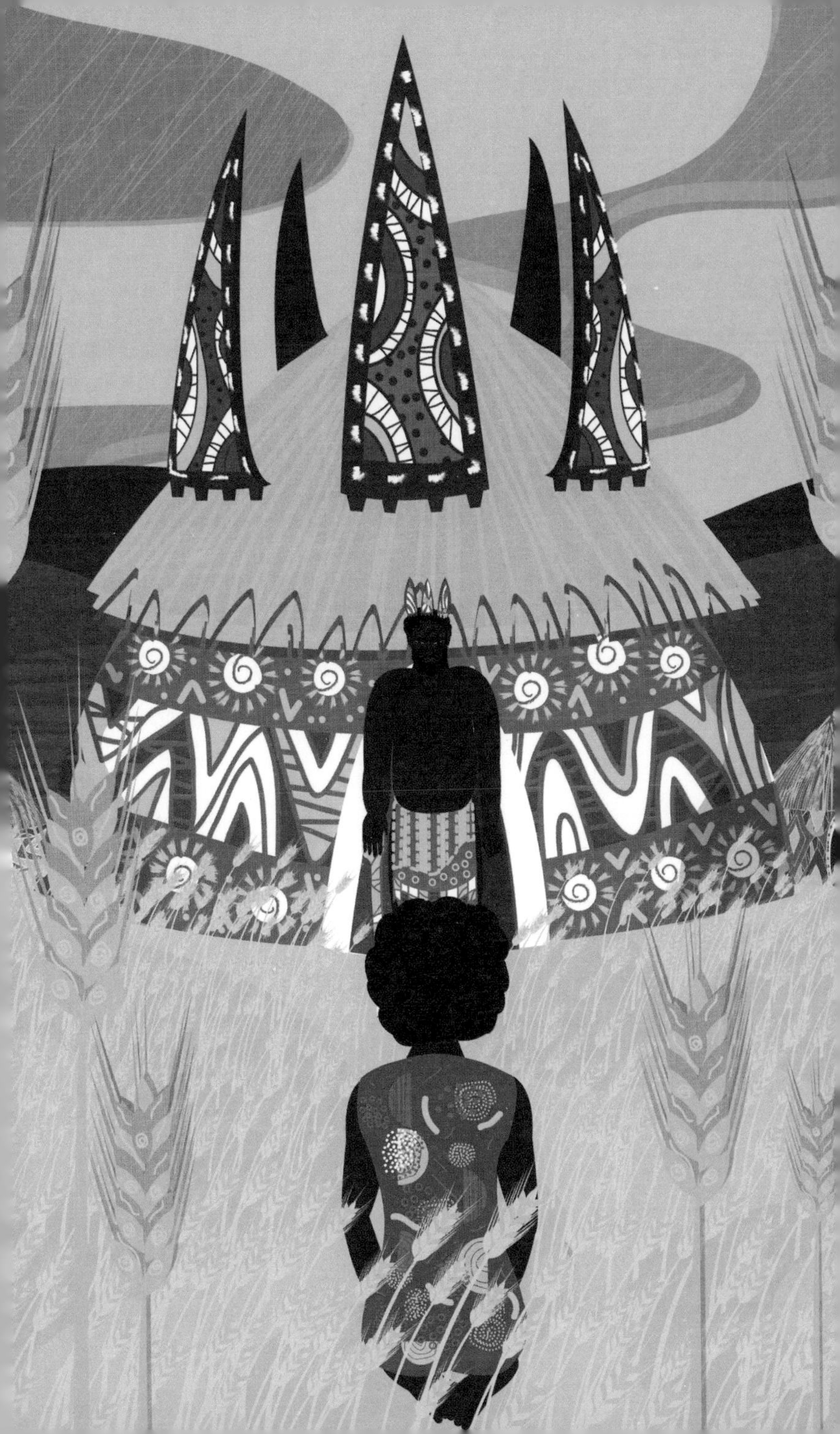

The crops grew tall and were ready to eat, but Yennenga did not cut them. Then the crops started to die.

"Yennenga, cut the crops! They are dying and our people must eat!" said King Nedega.

"No," she answered. "Our people are the same as these crops. They will die, too, without help. But you tell me no. I cannot help them!"

The king was very angry. He put Yennenga in prison because he wanted her to think differently. But Yennenga did not change.

Then one dark night months later, a warrior friend came to her door. "Princess, you must run away from here," he said, quietly. "I want to help you." He gave her some men's clothes to wear and her own horse. Then they rode away together. The princess was sad to leave her family and her people.

Yennenga and her warrior friend rode for many days. They arrived in a forest near a Malinke village.

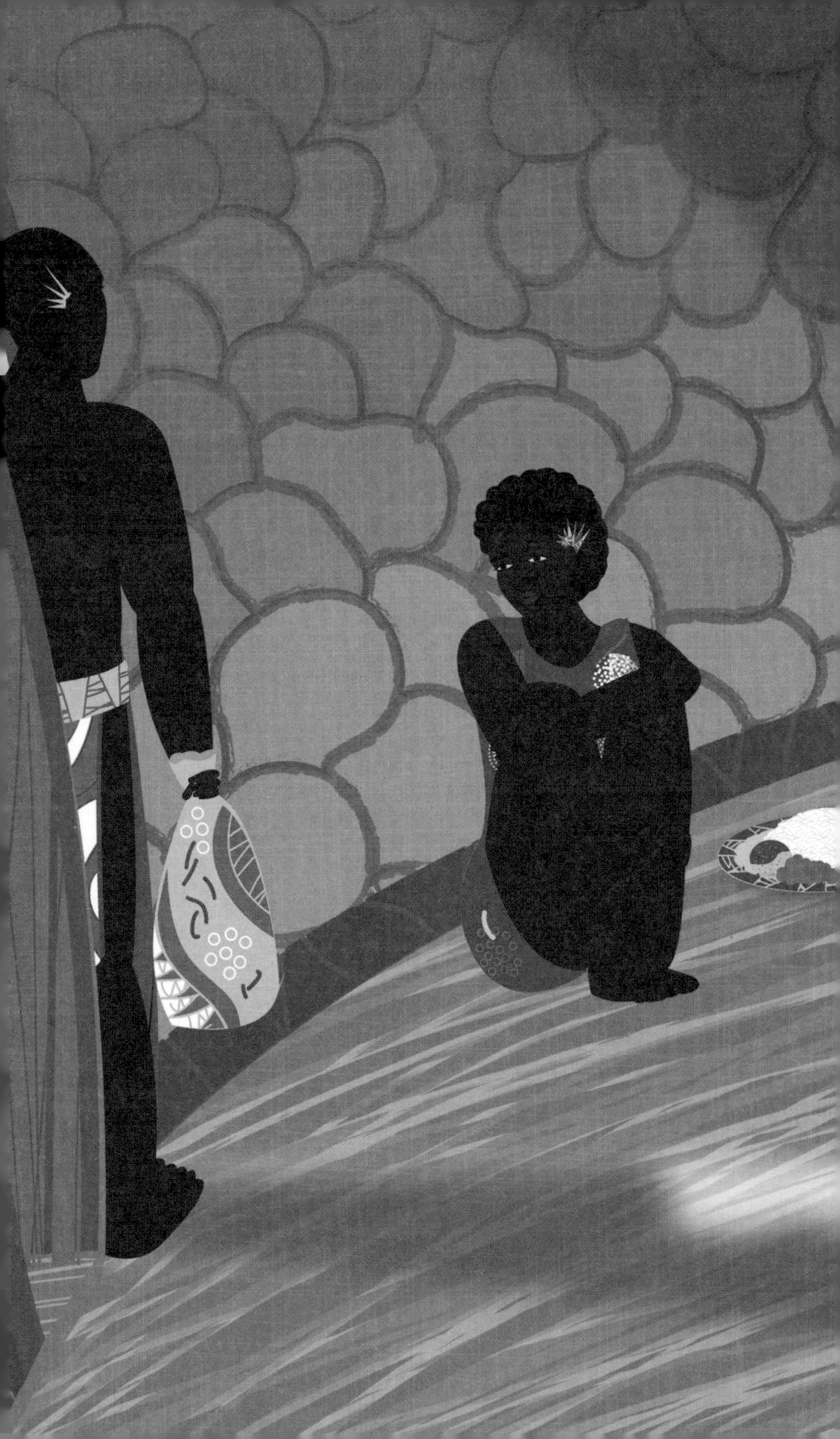

A group of Malinke warriors came with bows and arrows. The princess and her friend were brave, but there were too many warriors. The men fought her friend and killed him. The princess was very angry, and she rode at the warriors with her sword. Yennenga was a wonderful warrior, and she killed all the men.

The princess was very tired after the fight, but she rode on. She rode for many days and many nights.

"I am so thirsty," she said to her horse. "I don't know this place. There are no rivers here."

They came to another forest and Yennenga rode into it. Her eyes were heavy, and she was very tired and hungry. She fell from the horse into two kind, strong arms. Those arms helped her and put her on the ground of the dark forest. Her eyes closed, and she slept for a long time.

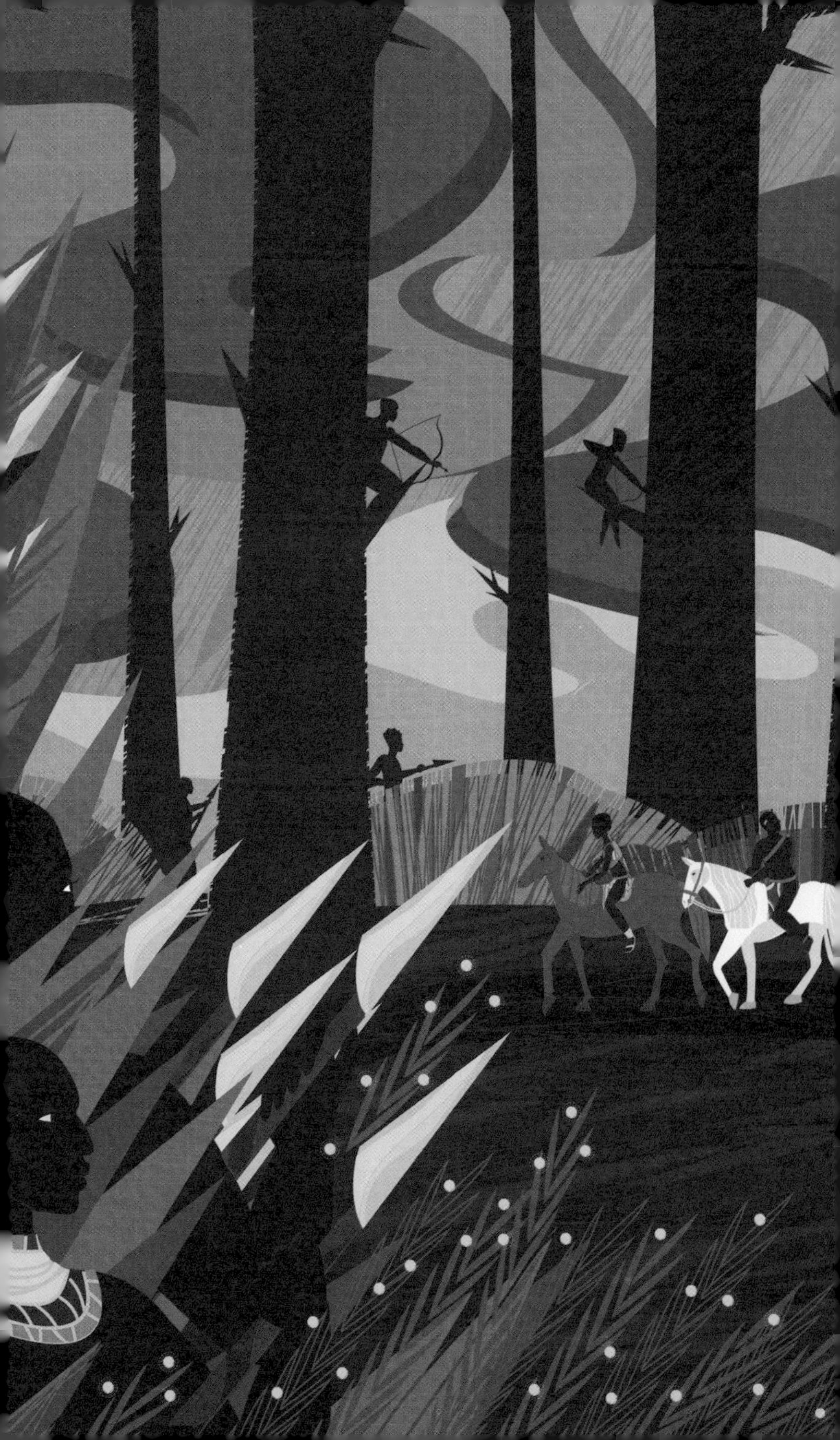

The next morning, Yennenga opened her eyes and there was a warm fire in front of her. A young man sat by it.

"My name is Riale," he said. "I'm a **hunter**. I find and kill elephants in the forest. I don't have much food, but please eat with me."

Riale was a kind man and Yennenga liked him. They talked about lots of different things and enjoyed being together. After some weeks, Yennenga started to love Riale.

"I want to stay with you, Riale," she said. "But I must tell you something. I am the princess of the Dagbon Kingdom. My father's angry with me and I can't go home again."

"I'll look after you and we will be happy together here," said Riale.

They married, and they had a son called Ouedragogo. He was brave, intelligent and kind. Many years later, Ouedragogo started the Mossi Kingdom. And Princess Yennenga, a wonderful warrior and kind woman, was the new mother of the Mossi Kingdom.

Rostam and his horse Rakhsh

Rostam the warrior was tall, strong and brave. His father Zal was a famous warrior. He looked after King Kavus, the king of Persia. One day, Zal gave his young son a beautiful horse called Rakhsh.

"Be brave," said Zal, "Persia is your country and you must always be strong for the king."

There were no battles in Persia for many years, but then things changed. King Kavus wanted to be king of Mazandaran, the kingdom of **demons**. Zal was an old man now and did not fight in battles any more. But he talked to the king.

"Please don't do this," he said. "You cannot fight demon magic with a man's sword!" But the king did not listen. He travelled to Mazandaran with his many warriors and there was a big battle. Sadly, the king did not win and many warriors died. The White Demon, one of the warriors of Mazandaran, put the king in prison and **blinded** him. After many weeks, someone brought a message to Zal from the king.

Rostam said, "I will go to Mazandaran."

"But you don't fight in battles!" said his father.

"You are old and you cannot fight now," said Rostam. "I will be fine. I have Rakhsh."

Rostam and Rakhsh rode for days and days through the forest. It was a dark place and it was full of problems for Rostam. One night, he was asleep by the fire and his horse was awake. A big lion walked towards Rostam. Rakhsh ran at the animal. It turned and it went away.

"Thank you, Rakhsh!" said Rostam. "We are strong together."

They rode on, but there were no rivers and no water to drink. The weather was hot, and they were very thirsty.

"Please, **God**. Give us water or we will die," said Rostam. Then he opened his eyes, and saw a sheep. It started walking and Rostam and Rakhsh went after it. After many hours, they arrived at a river. They were very happy because now they could drink and sleep.

Rostam rode on, and the next night they stopped and slept. In the middle of the night something happened and Rakhsh opened his eyes. There was a small but angry **dragon** next to him. Rakhsh tried to wake Rostam up, but the dragon quickly walked away.

"There's nothing here!" said Rostam to his horse. "Why did you wake me up? I want to sleep."

An hour later, the dragon was there again. This time Rostam woke up, and he killed the dragon.

"Thank you, Rakhsh!" he said. "You were right. There *was* something here."

The next day they rode on, and they found a wonderful place in a forest. There was water and lots of good things to eat. Rostam was very happy, and he started to sing.

An old **witch** lived in the forest. "His singing is beautiful!" she thought. "I want to put that man in prison. Then I can hear him sing every day."

She changed into a young woman and visited
Rostam that evening.

Rostam was a kind man, and he **offered** the woman some food. Then he said, "God, thank you for this food."

The name of God broke the witch's magic. She changed into an old woman again and Rostam quickly killed her with his sword.

The next evening, Rostam and Rakhsh arrived at a farm. Rostam was very hungry, and he walked into the farm. He wanted to eat a little of the crops.

"Stop!" shouted Olad, the farmer. "Don't steal my crops!"

Then Rostam told Olad his story.

"Please help me to get to Mazandaran," Rostam said.

"All right. I'll take you there," said Olad.

After a long time, they arrived at the great walls of Mazandaran. Rostam started to fight, and he killed the warriors there. Then he went inside and found the prison of King Kavus.

"I want to help you," he told King Kavus. The king was very happy to see him.

"Then you must find and kill the White Demon for me," said the king.

"Cut the demon and take some of his red blood. Bring it to me and I will be able to see again."

"The White Demon lives in a cave," said Olad to Rostam. "I understand him. He fights well. But you must wait until he laughs. He won't be able to fight well then."

The next morning, Rostam rode to the White Demon's cave and walked bravely inside. The demon was as big as a mountain.

"I am going to kill you!" shouted Rostam.

"You're only a man. You can't kill *me*!" said the demon. And then he laughed. Now he was *not* ready to fight and Rostam quickly killed him with a sword. Rostam then caught some of the demon's blood in a cup. He took the blood to the prison and opened the door. King Kavus came out and the demon's blood helped him to see again.

"Let's go home to our kingdom now," said Rostam. But King Kavus did not want to go home.

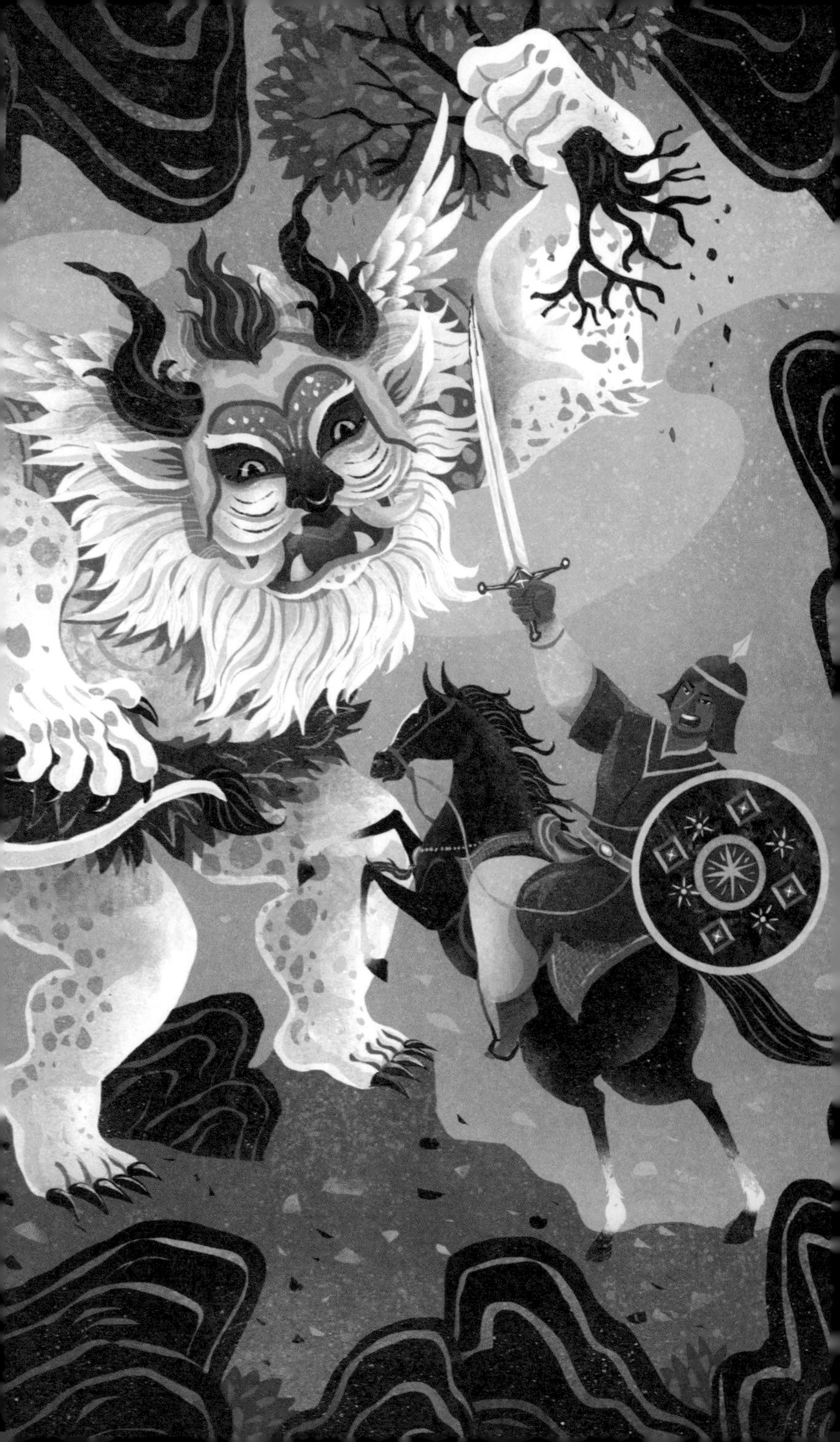

"No," he said. "I want to win the kingdom of Mazandaran." And he went to see the king of the demons.

"My brave warrior killed your White Demon and many of your other warriors," he shouted. "Give your kingdom to me, or he will kill you, too!"

The demon king said no. Then Rostam rode on Rakhsh and started to fight. But the demon king quickly changed into a mountain.

"You cannot kill me now!" he said. But brave Rostam hit the mountain with his axe.

"I will not stop!" shouted Rostam, angrily. "I'll use my axe until you die!"

The demon king was frightened. "Stop!" he said, and he gave his kingdom to Rostam and King Kavus.

"Olad," said Rostam. "The Mazandaran Kingdom is now ours, but will you be its king?" Olad was a good man, and he was happy to be the king. And

Kavus, Rostam and Rakhsh went home to their people to tell them the good news.

Shakuntala and the gold ring

There was a **wise man** called Rishi Kanva. He lived in India, near the Himalayan mountains. One day, he found a baby girl by the river Ganga. He took her home and called her Shakuntala. She was a friendly, brave child and Rishi taught her to sing and dance.

"You are a young woman now," Kanva said years later. "Try to be kind and look after people. And remember, always have hope."

One afternoon, Shakuntala was in the forest, and she saw a frightened deer. It ran towards her. Then a hunter on a horse arrived. The hunter wanted to kill the deer.

"Please don't kill it!" Shakuntala shouted, and she moved in front of the deer.

"You can't stop me," answered the hunter, angrily. "I am Dushyanta, King of Hastinapura. Everything in this forest is mine."

They married that day in the forest. Shakuntala took some grass and made a ring for her new husband. And the king gave Shakuntala his gold ring. There was a picture of him on it.

The next day, King Dushyanta went home to Hastinapura. Shakuntala got ready to go to Hastinapura, too.

Then a wise man called Durvasa came to Shakuntala's house because he was very thirsty and hungry. He shouted to her, but Shakuntala did not hear him. He shouted again, but she did not come.

"This is very bad!" Durvasa shouted, very loudly now. Shakuntala heard him and came quickly, but it was too late. The wise man was angry.

"You only think about your new husband! I am going to put a **curse** on you. Your husband will now forget you!"

Shakuntala was very angry and sad about this. She quickly offered the wise man food and drink, and she said sorry.

The wise man slowly stopped feeling angry. "I can't change the curse now," he said. "But something can break it. Show your husband something of his. Then he will remember you."

Shakuntala looked at the gold ring on her finger. "Can it break the curse?" she thought.

Weeks later, Shakuntala visited her father. She told him about the wise man and the curse.

"I'm going to have King Dushyanta's baby, too," she said.

"You must tell him," Rishi said. "Let's go to your husband tomorrow."

They walked for days until they arrived at the river Ganga. There, they went on a boat across the water. Shakuntala was tired, and she washed her face with some river water. She did not see it, but the gold ring went down into the water.

Later that day, they arrived at King Dushyanta's palace. Shakuntala asked to see the king.

"Who are you?" Dushyanta asked her. He did not remember her because of the curse.

"I am your queen. Look," said Shakuntala. She held up her hand, but the ring was not there! She could not break the curse without the ring!

"You are not my queen," said the king. "Go away."

Shakuntala and her father went home. "I must find the ring," thought Shakuntala.

Rishi and Shakuntala went back to the river and went across in the boat again. "I understand now!" thought Shakuntala. "I washed my face in the river. Did the gold ring go down in the water?"

"This river goes out into the sea," said her father. "You will never see that ring again."

"But Father, there's always hope," said Shakuntala. "I *will* find that ring."

Shakuntala and her father went home to the forest. Months later, Shakuntala had a baby boy, and she called him Bharatha.

"My son is a prince," said Shakuntala. "And I will teach him to be a prince." Bharatha was a kind, brave person – the same as his mother.

Many summers later, a fish found the gold ring in the river. It was hungry and it ate the ring. Then a man caught the fish and cut it open. He found the gold ring inside it.

"This ring has a picture of the king on it!" said

the man. He quickly went to the palace with it.

The man gave the ring to the king and it broke the curse.

"I remember now!" said the king. "Shakuntala is my queen!" The king bought lots of beautiful clothes for Shakuntala and got his horse ready.

He rode for a long time and came to a forest. There he found a young boy and a baby lion. The boy played with the lion and laughed.

"You aren't frightened!" said the king.

"Of course not," answered the boy and smiled.

"What's your name?" asked the king.

"I'm Bharatha," he said. "And one day I'll be the king of this forest!"

The king was very happy. "This boy is my son!" he thought. Then Shakuntala came out of the trees and saw her son with King Dushyanta.

"Dushyanta!" she cried. "I always hoped for this! You remember me!"

King Dushyanta went home to Hastinapura with

his queen and his prince. There was a big party and the people loved Shakuntala. And many years later, Prince Bharatha was the king of Hastinapura and his mother was very happy.

During-reading questions

SUNDIATA THE LION KING

1 Who comes to the palace and sees King Konaté?
2 What does Sundiata's mother give him?
3 Why is Dankaran very angry?
4 Who is Sumanguru, and why is he strong?
5 What does Sumanguru change into, and where does he go?

YENNENGA AND THE MOSSI KINGDOM

1 What does Yennenga do every day?
2 What things does Yennenga learn to use?
3 Why is the king angry?
4 Who comes to the prison, and why does he come?
5 Who helps Yennenga in the forest?
6 What is Yennenga's son called?

ROSTAM AND HIS HORSE RAKHSH

1 Zal does not fight in battles now. Why?
2 What animal helps Rostam to find water?
3 Who wants to put Rostam in prison? Why?
4 Rostam visits a farm. Why does he do this, and who stops him?
5 What does King Kavus want Rostam to bring him? Why does he want this?
6 What does the demon king change into?

1 What animal does Shakuntala see in the forest, and how does she help it?

2 What three things does Shakuntala want from King Dushyanta?

3 Who comes to visit Shakuntala, and what bad thing does he do?

4 Look at the picture on page 51. What is Shakuntala saying, do you think?

5 What does the fish eat in the river?

6 Dushyanta talks to a boy in the forest and thinks, "This boy is my son!" Why does he think this, do you think?

After-reading questions

1 Look at your "Words I need to learn" list from "Before-reading question 2" on page 6. Use each word in a sentence.

2 Do you like the people in these four stories? Complete these sentences.

I like ... because ...

I do not like ... because ...

3 King Nedega taught Yennenga to be kind, and Rishi Kanva told Shakuntala, "Try to be kind and look after people." Are Sundiata, Yennenga, Rostam and Shakuntala kind? What kind things do they do, do you think?

4 Life is often very difficult for Sundiata, Yennenga, Rostam and Shakuntala. Which of them has the most difficult life, do you think? Why?

Exercises

1 Choose the correct word or phrase to complete these
sentences in your notebook.

1 Konaté is the king of the Manding *kingdom* / **palace**
in Africa.

2 Dankaran goes to see a **fortune teller** / **sorcerer**.

3 Sundiata wants to **change** / **win** the game at
King Mansa's palace.

4 Sundiata is strong and **brave** / **angry**.

5 Sumanguru's father lives in a **cave** / **village**.

2 Complete these sentences in your notebook with the
correct form of the verb.

Sundiata ¹......*lived*...... (**live**) in Manding, in Africa. One day,
his father King Konaté ²............ (**die**). Because Sundiata's brother
Dankaran wanted ³............ (**be**) the next king, he planned ⁴............
(**kill**) Sundiata. But Sundiata ⁵............ (**leave**) Manding. Years later,
Sundiata ⁶............ (**come**) to Manding and ⁷............ (**fight**) the
sorcerer Sumanguru. Sundiata ⁸............ (**win**) the fight and was
then the new king.

3 **Are these sentences *true* or *false*? Write the correct answers in your notebook.**

1 Yennenga's brothers ask Yennenga to train harder. ....*false*...........

2 Yennenga goes into battle with her brothers.

3 King Nedega does not want crops outside his door.

4 Yennenga falls from her horse because she is tired.

5 Riale hunts deer, sheep and elephants in the forest.

4 **Complete these sentences in your notebook with the correct form of the adjective..**

1 Yennenga is a ....*better*........... (**good**) rider than her brothers.

2 On her horse, Yennenga can go as .... (**fast**) as the wind.

3 Yennenga is the .... (**fast**) rider in the Dagbon Kingdom.

4 Yennenga is .... (**strong**) than her brothers.

5 King Nedega's sons are not as .... (**kind**) as Yennenga.

5 **Write the correct answers in your notebook.**

Example: *1 – b*

1 Zal, a famous warrior, looks after *the king of Persia.*

   a a horse

   b the king of Persia

   c the kingdom of Persia

2 In the forest at night, Rakhsh frightens ....

   a a lion, a sheep and a dragon

   b a lion, a dragon and a witch

   c a lion and a dragon

3 Rostam meets a .... called Olad.

   a farmer

   b warrior

   c demon

4 Rostam uses .... on the demon king.

   a a bow and arrow

   b a sword

   c an axe

6 Complete these sentences in your notebook, using the prepositions from the box.

for	into	in	with	at

1 The White Demon puts King Kavus ....*in*........ prison.
2 Rostam thanks God .... the food they are going to eat.
3 After many hours of walking, Rostam and Rakhsh arrive .... a farm.
4 The demon king changes .... a mountain.
5 Rostam hits the mountain .... his axe.

SHAKUNTALA AND THE GOLD RING

7 Put these sentences in the correct order in your notebook.

a .... Shakuntala and Dushyanta are married.
b .... Shakuntala stops a man from killing a deer.
c .....*1*..... A wise man called Rishi Kanva finds a baby by a river.
d .... A man fishing at the river finds the gold ring.
e .... Dushyanta does not remember Shakuntala.
f .... Dushyanta remembers Shakuntala and meets his son for the first time.
g .... The gold ring falls into a river.

8 **Write the correct question word. Then answer the questions in your notebook.**

| Why | Where | How | What | Who |

1 ....*Who*.... wants to kill the deer?
Dushyanta wants to kill the deer.
2 .... many things does Shakuntala ask Dushyanta for?
3 .... does King Dushyanta live?
4 .... is the wise man Durvasa angry with Shakuntala?
5 .... does Shakuntala teach her son, Bharatha, to be?

Project work

1 You are one of these people. Write a diary page.
   • Sundiata's mother sees Sundiata walk on his seventh birthday.
   • Yennenga goes into prison.
   • Rostam arrives at the great walls of Mazandaran.
   • Shakuntala sees Dushyanta in the forest with Bharatha.
2 Which of the four stories do you like the best? Write a review of that story.
3 Are Sundiata, Yennenga, Rostam and Shakuntala happy at the end of their stories, do you think? Write about each person.
4 Talk with a friend. One person is Sundiata, Yennenga, Rostam or Shakuntala, and the other person asks questions about their life.

An answer key for all questions and exercises can be found at **www.penguinreaders.co.uk**

Glossary

battle (n.)
a very big fight with many people

blind (v.)
If someone *blinds* you, then you cannot see.

brave (adj.)
A *brave* person is not frightened.

broke (v.) present tense: **break**
went into small parts

cave (n.)
a place in the side of a hill or mountain. People lived in *caves*.

crops (n.)
Crops are plants. They grow on a farm and people eat them.

curse (n.)
In stories, a *witch* or a *sorcerer* puts a curse on someone. Then the person's life is very bad.

demon (n.)
in stories, a very bad person. A *demon* uses *magic*.

dragon (n.)
in stories, a large animal. A *dragon* can fly, and fire comes out of its mouth.

fortune teller (n.)
A *fortune teller* tells you about your life. For example, "you will meet an important person, you will marry, or something bad will happen".

God (pr. n.)
God is the most important thing in many people's lives. People talk to *God* because they want something.

hunter (n.)
A *hunter* kills animals for food.

kingdom (n.)
A king has a *kingdom*. He *looks after* it. He is the most important person in it. Everyone in the *kingdom* must listen to him.

look after (phr. v.)
to help a person, animal or thing

magic (n.)
A *witch* or a *sorcerer* does *magic*. Then strange things happen. Sometimes these strange things are good and sometimes they are bad.

offer (v.)
You *offer* something to a person. You say, "Do you want this?"

palace (n.)
a big, beautiful house

prince (n.)
the son of a king or queen

princess (n.)
the daughter of a king or queen

royal family (n.)
a king, a queen and their family

sorcerer (n.)
In stories, a *sorcerer* is a bad man.
He uses *magic* to do bad things.

train (v.)
You *train* people or animals. You
teach them to do things.

win (v.)
to be the best or first in a game

wise man (n.)
A *wise man* knows a lot about
people and the world.

witch (n.)
In stories, a *witch* is an ugly, bad
person. She wears black clothes
and uses *magic* to do bad things.